# DOUBT

THE FORTEAN SOCIETY MAGAZINE

Vol. II Whole Number 40


# ALL "SAUCERS"

EDITED BY

TIFFANY THAYER

35c. 2/— in Great Britain

# ALL "SAUCERS" Doubt. THE FORTEAN SOCIETY MAGAZINE. Vol. II. Number. 40.

Tiffany Thayer
Editor

Adapted By
Alfred Steber

SAUCERIAN PUBLISHER
Original Sources in Ufology

ISBN: 978-1-955087-35-3

# Prologue to the Edition

The Fortean Society was started in the United States in 1931 during a meeting held in the New York flat of American writer Charles Hoy Fort, in order to promote his ideas. The Fortean Society was primarily based in New York City. Its first president was Theodore Dreiser, an old friend of Charles Fort, who had helped to get his work published. Founding members of the Fortean Society included Tiffany Thayer, Booth Tarkington,Ben Hecht, Alexander Woollcott and many of New York's literati such as Dorothy Parker. But "Fort had his share of detractors. His friend H. L. Mencken said his head was filled with 'Bohemian mush'". Other members included Vincent Gaddis, Ivan T. Sanderson, A. Merritt, Frank Lloyd Wright and Buckminster Fuller. The first six issues of the Fortean Society's newsletter *Doubt* were each edited by a different member, starting with Theodore Dreiser. Tiffany Thayer thereafter took over editorship of subsequent issues. Thayer began to assert extreme control over the society, largely filling the newsletter with articles written by himself, and excommunicating the entire San Francisco chapter, reportedly their most active, after disagreements over the society's direction, and forbidding them to use the name Fortean. During World War II, for example, Thayer used every issue of "Doubt" to espouse his politics. Particularly, he frequently expressed opposition to Civil Defense, going to such lengths as encouraging readers to turn on their lights in defiance to air raid sirens. In contrast to the spirit of Charles Fort, he not only dismissed flying saucers as nonsense, but also dismissed the atomic bomb as a hoax.

The Fortean Society Magazine (also called *Doubt*) was published regularly until Thayer's death in Nantucket, Massachusetts in 1959, when the society went on hiatus and the magazine came to an end. Writers Paul and Ron Willis, publishers of "Anubis", acquired most of the original Fortean Society material and revived The Fortean Society as the International Fortean Organization (INFO) in 1961. INFO continues to this day and went on to incorporate in 1965, publish[citation needed]"The INFO Journal: Science and the Unknown" for over 35 years and created the first conference dedicated to the work and spirit of Charles Fort, the annual FortFest.

The original magazin Doubt and society were not connected to the present-day magazine Fortean Times, created by a British Fortean and long-time correspondent to Paul Willis, Bob Rickard, who encouraged Willis to publish.

Much of the Fortean Society material including material from Fort, Dreiser and Hecht, excepting many of the notes of Charles Fort which were donated to the New York Public Library as a collection, was incorporated into the International Fortean Organization (INFO).

Tiffany Ellsworth Thayer (March 1, 1902 – August 23, 1959) was an American actor, writer, and one of the founding members of the Fortean Society.

Born in Freeport, Illinois, Thayer quit school at age 15 and worked as an actor, reporter, and used-book clerk in Chicago, Detroit, and Cleveland. When he was 16, he toured as the teenaged hero in the Civil War drama The Coward. Thayer first contacted American author Charles Fort in 1924. In 1926, Thayer moved to New York City to act, but soon spent more time writing.

In 1931 Thayer co-founded the Fortean Society in New York City to promote Fort's ideas. Primarily based in New York City, the Society was headed by first president Theodore Dreiser, an old friend of Fort who had helped to get his work published. Early members of the original Society in New York City included Booth Tarkington, Ben Hecht, Alexander Woollcott, and H. L. Mencken. The first 6 issues of Doubt, the Fortean Society's newsletter, were each edited by a different member, starting with Dreiser. Thayer thereafter took over editorship of subsequent issues. Thayer began to assert extreme control over the society, largely filling the newsletter with articles written by himself, and excommunicating the entire San Francisco chapter, reportedly their largest and most active, after disagreements over the society's direction, and forbidding them to use the name Fortean.

During World War II, Thayer used every issue of *Doubt* to espouse his politics. He celebrated the escape of Gerhart Eisler, and named Garry Davis an Honorary Fellow of the Society for renouncing his American citizenship. Thayer frequently expressed opposition to Civil Defense, going to such lengths as encouraging readers to turn on their lights in defiance of air raid sirens. In contrast to the spirit of Charles Fort, he dismissed not only flying saucers as nonsense but also the atomic bomb as a hoax by the US government.

Thayer also wrote several novels, including the bestseller Thirteen Women which was filmed in 1932 and released by RKO Radio Pictures. Many of his novels contained elements of science fiction or fantasy, including Dr. Arnoldi about a world where no-one can die.

In the profile in Twentieth Century Authors, Thayer was described as "an atheist, an anarchist – in philosophy a Pyrrhonean– and regrets the legitimacy of his birth." He listed his hobbies as painting, fencing, and book collecting.

The Fortean Society Magazine (also called *Doubt*) was published regularly until Thayer's death in Nantucket, Massachusetts in 1959, aged 57, when the society and magazine came to an end. The magazine and society are not connected to the present-day magazine *Fortean Times.*

Writers Paul and Ron Willis, publishers of Anubis, acquired most of the original Fortean Society material and revived the Society as the International Fortean Organization (INFO) in the early 1960s. INFO went on to incorporate in 1965, publish a widely respected magazine, The INFO Journal: Science and the Unknown, for more than 35 years and created the world's first, and most prestigious, conference dedicated to the work and spirit of Charles Fort, the annual FortFest which continues to this day.

Alfred Steber

Saucerian Publisher

# DOUBT

**The Fortean Society Magazine**

*Edited by* TIFFANY THAYER
*Secretary of the*
FORTEAN SOCIETY
Box 192 Grand Central Annex
New York City
1931 A D = the year 1 F S
We use the Fortean 13-month calendar
Membership available to all
Annual dues $2.00
Dues in Sterling countries 8/—
In ENGLAND address
Eric Frank Russell
3, Dale Hey,
Hooton, Cheshire
In ITALY address:
Prince Boris de Rachewiltz
Castello d'Brunnenburg
Tirolo d'Merano
(Bolzano) Italy

For the addresses of Fortean centers in India, the Orient, Scandinavia, Germany, Mexico, South America, South Africa, Australia and New Zealand, apply to the Secretary.

DOUBT is on sale in principal cities of the world at 35c per copy, in Great Britain 2/—. Ask your bookseller to get it.

DOUBT is in principal Public Libraries, and many universities have complete files.

Ask us for list of back numbers still available.

All illustrations in DOUBT, unless otherwise credited, are the work of L M F S Art Castillo.


## SAUCERS ETCETERA

In the following digest of data received Your Secretary has made a conscientious effort to determine the source of the original story, from its context, divorced from semantics. As a former reporter, former publicity man, advertising man and sometime master of word-twistery, he feels rather competent to take the syntax apart.

The digest is divided into three sections. 1. Objects the papers called "saucers". 2. Objects the paper called "meteors". 3. Objects the papers did not know what to call, but refrained from calling either "saucers" or "meteors".

Some duplication may have crept in, but the aim has been to supplement the "saucer" data which appeared in DOUBT No. 23, No. 24, and No. 27, and to bring it up to date.

The statement is that "flying saucers" or "flying discs" or "flying disks" were the subject of "news" stories as follows:

### 1947 = 17 FS

July 4, Cincinnati *Enquirer*, UP. Reference is to a letter in the San Francisco *Chronicle*, signed Ole. J. Sneide, alleging that the "saucers" were "space ships from older planets".

July 10, Cincinnati *Times-Star*, AP. Man named Long in Van Nuys, Calif., found something in his garden.

Same date, INS, New York. Walter Winchell is quoted in favor of "belief". Alleged that something "went though the supersonic wall where it was traveling in space ahead of itself".

Aug 29. Two staff members of the Cincinnati *Enquirer* reported lights in the sky. The news services appear not to have picked the story up for their member-papers.

Nov. *Amazing Stories*, on its back cover, cites a sighting off Cape Race, Nov. 12, 1887.

### 1948 = 18 FS

Jan. *Amazing Stories*, on its back cover, cites a sighting over Greer, Idaho, Feb 5, 1910.

Mar 15. NSL, Union County, N. J. Flash and blast.

June 27, *Idaho Daily Statesman*, by Dave Johnson. An "anniversary" article stating that the "mystery" was one year old as of June 24.

July 25, UP. Philadelphia *Bulletin* and Philadelphia *Inquirer*, referred to what was reported in Atlanta, Ga., by two Eastern Air Line pilots. The same story, reported by AP, was in the Victoria, British Columbia, *Daily Times* the previous day. It was sent to us by Kenneth Arnold (MFS).

July 26, Los Angeles *Daily News*, ran a UP follow-up story, complete with posed Acme photo.

October 3, *Idaho Sunday Statesman*, Boise printed an AP despatch from Fargo, N.D. The story was reported by "a National Guard fighter pilot", and it was sent to us by Kenneth Arnold (MFS).

### 1949 = 19 FS

Jan 3 Seattle *Times* editorialized on the coincidence the the *Saturday Evening Post* and *True Magazine* had published "saucer" stories simultaneously with pronouncements from "The Army Air Force".

Jan 23. "Special" to Portland or Astoria, Oregon, or Seattle, Wash., paper. Tillamook (Oregon) dateline. Local people saw "saucer". Story not picked up by news services.

Jan 31. Orlando (Fla) *Evening Star*, by-line of John M. Fleming. The news services did not pick it up.

Mar 8. AP. Seen near Klamath Falls (Oregon).

Mar 11. San Bernardino *Daily Sun*. Local people saw. News services did not pick up.

Mar 12. AP. Washington, D.C. The "armed services" (branch unspecified) has classified saucer data "along with information on atomic bombs and guided missiles".

Is everybody shuddering?

Mar 13. Minneapolis *Tribune*. Describes what would have been called a "meteor", seen locally, and wraps the story around the above squib about the "armed services" clamming up.

Mar 20. Eight days after it was handed out, the *Wyoming State Tribune* just got around to printing the fright piece from Washington.

April 3. A correspondent writing to the Minneapolis *Tribune* mentioned Charles Fort.

April 7. Washington, D. C. "The Air Force" clamped on more secrecy, and went to the trouble of telling INS, and the NYT (who told the Dallas, Texas, *Times-Herald* and God knows whom else) how quiet it was going to keep this stuff.

May. The Minneapolis *Star* editorialized upon

Walter Winchell (said to favor a Russ source) and BSRA (the crowd of spirit-communers in Calif which publishes double-talk about life on "other planes", not meaning airplanes, but levels of immateriality).

May 20. Pueblo Colo. *Star-Journal*. Sighting.

July 16. Chicago *Tribune*. Local viewers. Press services did not pick up.

July 24. Boise, Idaho. AP. Seven in formation. (This is in DOUBT No. 27, p. 416.)

July 28. Seattle *Post-Intelligencer*, UP. Seen near Puyallup, Wash. May or may not be same one reported in DOUBT No. 27, as seen in Burien, Wash.

Aug 31. The Chicago *Tribune* printed the AP yarn with its Los Angeles dateline of Aug 30, which is in DOUBT No. 27, p. 417, as "seen Aug 26". Officers of the White Sands, N.M., "proving grounds" gave out the story.

Sept 7. Los Angeles *Examiner*, also the *Times*. First peep of La Paz, climbing aboard the bandwagon. He was speaking to U of SC, and tied "saucers" to "meteors" so that confusion reigned in almost all reports for about two years.

Oct 3. *Saratogian*, Saratoga, N.Y. By-line of Charles W. Andrews. Story was not picked up by press services.

Oct 15. U of Minnesota *Daily*. An "explanation" over by-line of Duane Rasmussen.

Oct 15. AP and UP, Williamsport, Pa., dateline. "An Army officer today said . . . " etc.

Oct 18. AP. Omaha, Neb., dateline. "Lt so and so of Offut airforce base, said he saw . . ." etc.

Oct 26. AP, Buffalo dateline. "Deputy Sheriff so and so, said he saw . . . " etc.

Undated piece of a few days later reports "mysterious objects over Troy, N.Y. It was not picked up by news services.

Oct 31. AP Los Angeles. "A weird comet-like aircraft" reported by a pilot.

Nov 15. Buffalo *Courier-Express*, in Rollin Palmer's column, *Bandwagon*.

December issue, *American Astrology Magazine*, p. 21, a letter, "personal experience of an aviator with a flying disk in mid-air".

Dec. 12. UP, Victoria, B.C.

Dec 16. Seattle *Post-Intelligencer*. INS follow-up on the incident of Dec. 12.

Dec 22. AP, Indianapolis. Radio commentator Frank Edwards is quoted.

Then came KEYHOE.

Anyone who wishes may read, *The Flying Saucers are Real*, in the January, 1950, issue of *True Magazine*. Both AP and UP sent out long stories, digesting the article, and their member papers published it widely, Dec 27 and 28.

Simultaneously, "the Air Force" announced that it was dropping the investigation "after checking 375 rumors". AP and UP from Washington.

Dec 29. AP Hamlet, N.C. Pilots chased something, they said. Printed everywhere.

Dec 29. Dallas *Times-Herald*. "It was Venus."

Dec 29. UP, Winston-Salem. Different man says, "It was Venus".

Dec. 29. *Wyoming State Tribune*. Different explanation. Not picked up.

Dec 29. AP, Richmond, Va. Radio station broadcast a fiction about a "saucer" landing. People as far away as Oakland, Calif., and New Haven, Conn., took it seriously.

Dec 30. Charlotte, N.C. Local sighting reported, plus AP stories from Asheville, Albemarle, and Columbia, S.C.

Dec 31. Oakland, Calif. Correspondent in the *Post-Enquirer*.

## 1950 == 20 FS

Jan 1. A motion picture, "the Flying Saucer" opened at the Rialto, N.Y.C.

Jan 3. Dallas *News*. in a column, "Offhand", conducted by Ken Hand.

Jan 11. AP, Tucumcari, N.M.

Jan 11. Frank Scully, writing in *Variety*, asked "the Air Force" twenty questions. Scully was writing his book on "saucers" at the time. The book is not worth reading.

Jan 14, 17, 18, 20. In the Peoria (Ill.) *Star*, MFS Gomer Bath editorialized, sometimes mentioning Fort.

Jan 16. *Oregonian*, Portland. Local people saw light. News services did not pick up.

Jan 17. Los Angeles *Mirror*. Columnist Dick Williams took up Scully story, and again a week later.

Jan 19. INS, Spencer, Indiana. Reported by a local telephone operator. Our copy from Seattle.

Jan 26. "Special" to the *Daily Oklahoman*, from Denison, Texas. The ed of the Denison paper found a report of a "saucer" over Denison, Jan 25, 1878.

Jan 29. UP, Pittsburgh. Quotes a "former science editor of *Time*".

Feb 2. AP, Tucson, Ariz. Two Air Force captains said they pursued it.

Feb 3. San Bernardino, *Sun*. Ten-year old girl saw something.

Feb 6. Falmouth, Mass. Two pilots—one formerly of Navy—one Air Force—told Roger A. Murray they saw something. *Cape Cod Standard Times*.

Feb 8. AP, San Francisco. Reported by Lt. Comdr. J. L. Kraker of the Alameda Naval Air Station.

Feb 9. Reuters, Santiago, Chile. Reported by the Chilean Under Secretary for the Navy.

Feb 13. UP, Halifax, N.S. Reported by Capt. William Crowell. Doesn't say what he's "captain" of.

Feb 15. Copyright by Chicago *Tribune*. "A farmer and his wife" near Copenhagen, Denmark. Reprinted in Los Angeles, and Allen, Okla.

Feb (?) Los Angeles *Daily News*. Columnist Matt Weinstock scoffs at the story that an experimental balloon, sent up with a camera attached, photographed a space ship away up there.

Feb 23. UP, Santiago, Chile. A commander in the Chilean Navy claimed to have photos. Not reproduced in the Seattle *Times*.

Feb 23. INS, New York. Commander Robert B. McLaughlin of the USN is quoted. His article was in *True Magazine*.

Feb 23. AP, New York. Sent a digest of the same article to its member papers. Much is made of "sighting" near White Sands.

Reuters and UP also picked it up. It went around the world.

Feb. 27. Venice, Italy. Reuters. Disk over Caioggia.

Feb 28. Seattle *Times*, debunks story which it asserts was widely disseminated, but the debunking is the first record we have of it.

Feb 28. UP, Cambridge, Mass. Routine report by

Shapley of an object visible only in telescopes, but headlined by the N. Y. *Times*: "Strange, Fast What-Is-It Sighted in Northern Sky."

Mar 6. Orchard Park, Calif. Local viewer. News services did not pick up.

Mar 6. INS, Tunis, North Africa.

Mar 6. *Rocky Mountain News*. Local viewer. Not picked up.

Mar 6. AP, Gering, Neb. Reported by a policeman.

Mar 8. INS, Dayton, Ohio. An Air National Guard pilot reported that he chased something.

Mar 9. United Press Science Editor, Paul F. Ellis, sent out his syndicated column on this subject.

Mar 9. AP, Van Nuys, Calif. .Police told the reporters.

Mar 9. UP. Mexico City.

Mar 9. Ray L. Dimmick's story of the little man killed in a saucer-crash began in the Los Angeles *Mirorr*. It was picked up by INS, AP, UP, and was printed everywhere for three days, with alterations by Dimmick, some double-talk by spokesmen for the Mexican government, some credulity by Navy men and others.

In Denver, a U of Denver "basic science" class was addressed by a "saucer expert" provided for the occasion by a radio time salesman name George T. Koehler. Watch for that "expert". He turns up again.

Mar 10. AP, INS, and UP all sent out stories stating that the Air Force "discounted" Dimmick's account.

Mar 10. Orangeburg, S.C. All services picked up a reported sighting by a newspaper publisher and his editor.

Mar 11. UP. Salinas, Calif. The sheriff's office reported many phone calls.

Mar 11. *Bulletin*, Edmonton, Alberta, Canada. Local view of three. Not picked up by United States papers or services.

Mar 11. AP. Something seen on an astronomer's photographic plate exposed Mar 2.

Mar 11. AP. Beverly Hills. A restaurant had a table reserved for the little saucer pilot.

Mar 11. AP. Calexico, reported by the mayor, no less.

Mar 11. Los Angeles *Times*. Report of a local viewer is tied to a speech by "former Crown Prince Otto of Austria"—in Salem, Ohio—who is quoted as "thinking" the flying saucers are Russian map recording devices.

Mar 11. INS. Danbury, Conn. Local viewer.

Mar 12. Sunday. Los Angeles *Times*, ran an artist's drawing of his impression of a description, but the headlines surrounding the monstrosity read "Amateur Photographer Snaps Weird Disk in Sky". One full page is devoted to other ramifications and rehash of well known material. Technically, the *Times* committed no fraud, but an estimated nine-tenths of their readers were deceived.

Mar 12. AP. Washington, D.C. The Air Force had nothing to add to its report of the previous December.

Mar 13. *Rocky Mountain News*, Denver. Local viewers. Picked up next day by UP.

Mar 13. Science Service got in the act. Six possible "explanations" sent to its subscribers.

Mar 13. Andrew Bernhard, editor of the Pittsburgh *Post-Gazette* editorialized.

Mar 14. UP. Durango, Colorado, also Mexico City. Reported by "trained aircraft observers and meteorologists."

Mar 14. Chicago *Sun-Times*. Reported by a Canadian airplane pilot.

Mar 14. Chicago *Daily News*. Reported by a Du Quoin, Ill., polot, as seen Feb 22.

Mar 14. Manchester *Guardian*, editorialized.

Mar 15. UP. Blackfoot, Idaho.

Mar 15. Canadian Press (Service) Ottawa.

Mar 15. Canadian Press, Saskatoon.

Mar 15. San Bernardino, Calif., *Sun-Telegram*. Local viewers. Not picked up.

Mar 15. AP. Lima, Peru.

Mar. 16. Special to the Toronto *Daily Star*. Viewed at Delhi, Ontario. Not picked up.

Mar 16. UP and AP. St. Marys, Pa. Reported by "a technical director for a Washington (D.C.) medical instrument supply firm." Query: does his firm serve the armed services?

Mar 16. UP. Anna, Ill. Another "doctor".

Mar 17. UP. Mexico City. Movie camera may have caught. That is all.

Mar 17. UP. Mount Vernon, Wash.

Mar 18. UP. Erie, Pa.

Mar. 18. Chicago *Herald-American*. Meeting of the Chicago Rocket Society.

Mar 18. Havana, Cuba. Reported by pilot.

Mar 18. AP. Farmington, N.M. Reported by editor of paper .

Mar 18. INS. The Chancellor of Denver U was raising hell about that unidentified "expert" who lectured—as above. More to come.

Mar 18. Reuters. Seen near Torino, Italy. Not picked up by USA papers.

Mar 18. UP. "Air force spokesman said"—etc.

Mar 18. UP, Bursa, Turkey. Reported by "Mohammedan priests".

Mar 18. San Bernardino *Sun-Telegram* editorialized.

Mar 18. AP. Altoona. Remarkable resemblance between drawing made by medical instrument man and drawing formerly printed in True Magazine is mentioned by AP.

Mar 18. Philadelphia *Inquirer* quotes "an Air Force officer".

Mar 18. INS. Chattanooga, Tenn., and Dallas, Texas. One report by a "former B-29 gunner", another by a "Naval petty officer".

Mar 19. Unidentified paper in England printed report from Montevideo, Uruguay. Not picked up by USA services.

Mar 19. "Air Force" sent out another denial from Washington. Some papers printed it on Mar 20.

Mar 19. Newark *News*, reported local viewers at Rumson, N.J. Not picked up by services.

Mar 20. Toronto *Telegram*. "An RCAF veteran" reported. Not picked up by USA services.

Mar 20. Chicago *Tribune*. Local "former navy air photographer". Not picked up.

Mar 21. UP. Memphis. Reported by commercial pilot.

Mar 21. NANA sent its papers a piece by W. H. Shippen building up the "secrecy" of the Air Force as applied to our subject. Washington, D.C. dateline.

Mar 21. UP. New York. The regular publicity release on the "approach of Mars" was headlined *a la* saucer.

Mar 21. AP datelined the Memphis story from "Little Rock" Ark. Oakland (Calif) *Tribune*.

Mar 22. AP Lisbon. Reported by coast guards of North Portugal. "Scores" seen.

Mar 22. UP. Idyllwild, Calif. Reported by Air Force officers.

Mar 22. Chicago *Sun-Times* printed directions for photographing tin pie pans thrown in the air.

Mar 22. Berkeley, Calif. Lick Observatory spokesman is quoted, apparently on the initiative of an Oakland *Tribune* reporter. Story not picked up by services.

Mar 22. Chicago *Daily News*. "An air force intelligence officer disclaimed . . . " etc.

Mar 22. UP. New York. Mrs. Roosevelt invited airline pilots who reported sighting to appear with her on TV.

Mar 22. UP. Asiago, Italy. Reported by "doctors and lawyers".

Mar 22. UP. Toronto. The only clipping of this one we received is from the Paris edition of the N. Y. *Her-Trib*, which is also the source of the one next below.

Mar 23. UP. Belo Horizonte, Brazil. A man was jailed for selling "flying saucers".

Mar 23. Reuters, Buenos Aires. Police reported. Not picked up in USA.

Mar 23. UP. Laguana Beach, Calif. Reported by "an Army aircraft observer".

Mar 23. Dallas *News*. Local viewer at Farmersville, Texas. Story not picked up.

Mar 23. Hamilton (Ont) *Spectator*. Local viewer. Story not picked up.

Mar 23. Grand Forks (N.D.) *Herald*, on this date found space for the AP despatch from Little Rock, noted above. In other words, the stuff is not "news" but "filler".

Mar 24. Frank Brutto of the AP "Foreign Staff" wrote a piece from Rome on "Axis" experiments with "disks" in '42. It was printed all over the world.

Mar 24. Not to be outdone, UP sent out a report of sightings in Berlin, Vienna, Madrid and Lisbon.

Mar 24. Pittsburg *Sun-Telegraph* columnist George Dixon wrote humorously? of a landing.

Mar 24. AP. Springfield, Oregon. Local viewers.

Mar 25. UP Staff Correspondent William L. Hathaway interviewed Jean Piccard at U of Minn at Minneapolis.

Mar 25. AP. Brainard, Minn. Local viewer.

Mar 25. The movie "Flying Saucer" opened in Pittsburgh and got a lot of free space in local papers.

Mar 25. Reuters. Beirut. Reported by a pilot. Not picked up in USA.

Mar 25. An English paper, the *Recorder*, editorialized.

Mar 25. AP. New York. Reported by police.

Mar 25. *Humbolt Standard*, Eureka, Calif. Local viewer, U.S. Forestry worker. Not picked up.

Mar 26. UP. Vienna. Reported by police.

Mar 27. UP. Washington, D. C., reported by a clerk in the Congressional Library.

Mar 27. British UP. Cairo. Reported by an Egyptian pilot.

Mar 27. Hamilton (Ont) *Spectator* editorialized.

Mar 27. AP. Tulsa, Okla. Local viewers.

Mar 27. Chicago *Sun-Times* editorialized.

Mar 27. *Quick*. "Stalin's Politburo has named a commission of scientists to unearth the Muscovite who first beheld a flying caucer, circa 1903."

Mar 28. Dallas, Texas. Radio commentator Henry J. Taylor broadcast on the subject. AP release.

Mar 28. Pittsburgh *Post-Gazette*. Local viewers. Not picked up.

Mar 28. UP. Austin, Texas. University of Texas publicity release.

Mar 28. Reuters. Addis Ababa. Local viewers. No USA pick-up.

Mar 29. AP. Trinidad, Colo. Local viewers.

Mar 29. Oakland (Calif) *Tribune*. Local viewers. Not picked up.

Mar 29. UP. Leavenworth, Wash. Local viewers. "Playing tag with an Air Force bomber."

Mar 30. Toronto *Telegram*. Reported by "airport officials". Not picked up in USA.

Mar 31. Toronto *Globe and Mail*. Seen at Brantford (Ont). Not picked up in USA.

Mar 31. Toronto *Daily Star* editorialized.

Mar 31. Grand Forks (N. D. ) *Herald*. Local viewer. Not picked up.

Mar . UP. Nashville, Tenn. Local viewers.

Mar 31. AP. Minneapolis. Pronouncement issued by Maj. Gen. Richard C. Lindsay, deputy director of strategic planning for the joint chiefs of staff.

Mar 31. *Del Norte County Triplicate*. Local viewers around Crescent City, Calif. Not picked up.

Mar 31. AP. Sioux City, Ia. Reported by the Iowa Air National Guard.

Mar 31. UP. Greybull, Wyo. Local viewer.

Mar 31. UP. Washington, D.C. Story emanating from "the Navy".

Mar 31. Special to the Buffalo *Evening News*, from Niagara Falls, Ont. Local viewer. Not picked up.

Apr 1. AP. Feature for All Fool's Day, by Ed Creagh.

Apr 1. AP. Washington, D.C. Story about a magician by Harman W. Nichols.

Apr 1. St. Louis *Post-Dispatch*. Reported by "an Air Force veteran".

Apr 1. Hamilton (Ont) *Spectator*. Local viewer at Selkirk. Not picked up in USA.

Apr 1. AP. Frankfurt, Germany. Report of several humorous pieces in German papers and mags.

Apr 2. Reuters. London. Reported by the meteorological office.

Apr 2. A Sunday. St. Louis *Post-Dispatch* printed full page feature and resume, by Peter Wyden. Also, a sighting over Caracas, Venezuela, reported by a pilot.

Apr 2. *Daily Mail* (England). Feature story with New York dateline, by Richard Greenough. A resume.

Apr 2. UP. Monterey, Calif. Newspaper hoax said to have stirred up the town.

Apr 2. AP. Rome, Italy. A horse bolted at something it saw in the sky.

Apr 3. AP. Longmont, Colo. Reported by "a newspaper editor, a civil engineer and a retired banker".

Apr 3. AP. Washington, D.C. Quotes the *U. S. News and World Report*.

Apr 3. AP. London. Reported by the meterological office.

Apr 3. *Wyoming State Tribune*. At a meeting of the Cheyenne Toastmasters Club, they were discussed.

Apr 3. AP Wirephoto sent out a picture which was captioned in the Chicago *Herald-American*: "First photo reveals aviation secret—flying disc, picture of one-third scale model in National Advisory Committee laboratory."

Apr 3. Philadelphia *Bulletin*. Letter from a viewer.

Apr 4. AP. Key West. Truman's press secretary issued a statement on the subject.

Apr 4. UP. Washington, D.C. Pronouncement from the Air Force and Navy.

Apr 4. AP. Baltimore, Md. Speech by Dr. Charles Green, "a missile specialist with the General Electric Company."

Apr 4. Manchester *Guardian*. Seen over Pereira, Venezuela.

Apr 4. *Daily Mirror*, London. Local viewer. Not picked up in USA.

Apr 4. *Daily Mail*, London. Richard Greenough writes again.

Apr 4. UP. Henry J. Taylor broadcast over ABC, from New York.

Apr 4. AP Wirephoto sent out another photograph of something that the Navy says does not exist. The Navy issued the photo in 1946.

Apr 4. Reuters. Canberra, Australia. Sighting in Queensland, and announcement from the Australian patent office that they have plans for six, some 20 years old.

Apr 4. UP. Elizabeth, Ill. Local viewer.

Apr 5. Manchester *Guardian*. Editorial by Alistair Cooke, New York dateline.

Apr 5. UP. Washington, D. C. Pronouncements by Congressmen—one for, one against.

Apr 5. *Daily Mirror*, London. Humorous feature.

Apr 5. AP. Whitby, England, Local viewers.

Apr 5. Edmonton (Alberta) *Bulletin*. Reported by employee of Alberta Public Works Dept.

Apr 5. St. Louis *Globe-Democrat* editorialized.

Apr 6. Retuers. Asmara, Eritrea. Thousands viewed. Also in Buenos Aires, "thousands."

Apr 6. *Daily Mail* (England). Spoofing.

Apr 6. NEA, with photo. Kokomo, Ind. Local viewer.

Apr 7. INS, Chicago. Reported by a radio engineer.

Apr 7. Newark *Evening News* editorialized.

Apr 7. UP. Montvale, N.J. Willy Ley climbed on the bandwagon.

Apr 7. David Lawrence, syndicated column, dated Washington, D.C.

Apr 8. Moline, Ill. *Daily Dispatch*. Local viewers. Not picked up.

Apr 8. UP. Horseheads, N.Y. Gadget found, given to FBI.

Apr 8. AP. Upper Sandusky, O. Local newsmen saw.

Apr 8. INS. Gouverner, N.Y. Reported by a retired Navy Lieut.

Apr 8. (?). *West Jasper Place Review*, Alberta Canada, editorialized.

Apr 9. Springfield (Ill.) *News*. Local viewer.

Apr 9. Pittsburgh *Press*. Resume of local viewing. Not picked up.

Apr 10. UP. Boise, Idaho. Kenneth Arnold got back in the news.

Apr 10. UP. Amarillo, Texas. Boy aged 12 says he touched one before it flew away.

Apr 10. Oakland, Calif. *Post-Enquirer*. Letter from S. Johnson.

Apr 10. Toronto *Daily Star*. Local viewer at Oba, 150 miles N of Sault Ste. Marie. No pick up.

Apr 10. AP. Preston, England, Local viewers.

Apr 10. *Evening Standard*, England. Alleged photo of one over Majorca. Three seen in Henderson, Ky., by farmers. Photo by Heinrich Hausmann.

Apr 10. Liverpool *Echo* quotes the Yorkshire *Post*, alleging that a Bruges, Belgium, paper printed photos of one that landed in the middle of the town, and pix of Martians who walked out of it.

Apr 10. Pittsburgh *Post-Gazette*, column by Charles F. Danver. Local viewer, no pick up.

Apr 11. UP. Monterey, Calif. Reported by deputy sheriff.

Apr 11. New York *Times*. Quotes that same Henry J. Taylor, who says the Navy is sending them up near Minneapolis.

Apr 11. UP. York, Pa. Reported by State Highway workers.

Apr 11. UP. New York. Reported by former Air Force lieut.

Apr 12. UP. Buffalo. Reported by a Naval reservist.

Apr 12. UP. Neukirchen, Germany. Reported by American occupation officials.

Apr 12. AP. Moscow. The *New Times* is quoted as stating that saucer reports are spread "by American military authorities to squeeze larger appropriations out of American taxpayers".

Apr 12. UP. San Francisco. Army Intelligence orders agents to photograph any seen.

Apr 13. AP. Brussels, Belg. A mattress factory advertised for two saucers complete with crews.

Apr 13. UP. Dallas. Texas State Fair offered $50,000 for one.

Apr 13. Special to *World-Tele* from Montclair, N.J. Local viewers, not picked up.

Apr 13. Grand Forks (N.D.) *Herald*. Local viewer, not picked up.

Apr 14. UP. Monterey, Calif. Another inventor.

Apr 14. AP. Guaquil, Ecuador. Reported by a Senator!

Apr 14. AP. Rome. Reported over Palermo, Sicily, and Rome.

Apr 15. *Daily Telegraph* (London). Quotes David Lawrence who wrote that the US Army was going to "make public certain details" etc.

Apr 15. UP. Farmington, W. Va. Reported by a high school principal.

Apr 15. *Sunday Observer*, England. Feature resume by William Clark.

Apr 16. Pittsburgh *Post-Gazette*. Aero Club to discuss. Speeches by Air Force personnel.

Apr 16. Pittsburgh *Press*. Col by Gilbert Love, spoofing.

Apr 16. *Wyoming State Tribune* editorialized.

Apr 16. Des Moines, Ia., *Sunday Register*. Local viewers at Burlington. Not picked up.

Apr 17. London edition of the N. Y. *Herald* reports local viewers over Montmarte, Paris. Not picked up in USA.

Apr 17. Minneapolis *Star* editorialized. Also Li'l Abner cartooned.

Apr 17. David Lawrence column again.

Apr 17. *Newsweek*. Resume.

Apr 17. UP. Wellington, New Zealand, Local viewer.

Apr 17. UP. Dallas, Local inventor.

Apr 18. Marshalltown, Ia., *Times-Republican*. Local viewers at Fonda, one a former mayor of the place.

Apr 18. AP. Fort Worth, Texas. Reported by an Air Force veteran.

Apr 18. AP. Brussels, Belg. Auguste Piccard got on the bandwagon.

Apr 18. UP. Monterey, Calif. Deputy Sheriff again.

Apr 19. UP. Dallas. Reported by managing ed of Childress paper.

Apr 19. Washington State College, *Pullman*. Local viewers.

Apr 19. UP. Los Alamos, N.M. "More than 15 persons" saw—no two agreed on what was seen.

Apr 21. Pittsburgh *Post-Gazette*. "Silver foiled" thing found near Canonsburg, Pa.

Apr 21. Drew Pearson's syndicated col quotes Air Force denial.

Apr 21. AP. Salem, Oregon. Local photographer snaps one.

Apr 22. UP. Lufkin, Texas. Local viewer.

Apr 23. AP. Washington, D.C. Robert E. Geiger quotes Charles Fort.

Apr 23. San Francisco *Chronicle*. Local viewer, not picked up.

Apr 23. *Observer* (England) Charles Davy answers Mr. Clark—see above.

Apr 23. *Oregonian*. Portland, editorialized.

Apr 23. Salem, Oregon. Photo taken by Rand Hermann, Comas, Wash., March 12.

Apr 24. AP. Klamath Falls, again. Local viewers.

Apr 24. Denver *Post*, dug up a man who saw one July 3, 1949.

Apr 24. AP. Saigon, Indo-China. Reported by French Army officers.

Apr 25. Edmonton (Alb) *Bulletin*. Local viewer, Rocky Mountain House. Not picked up in USA.

Apr 25. CP. Vancouver, B.C. Local viewer. Picked up by AP next day.

Apr 26. UP. Norman, Okla. U of Okla prof sounds off.

Apr 26. Reuters. London. Quotes a Luebeck (Germany) report of sightings in Berlin and Lisbon, also predictions that same will occur "early next month" in Sweden!

Apr 26. CP. Sidney, B.C. Local viewer, not picked up.

Apr 26. Hartford (Conn) *Times*. Local viewer, not picked up.

Apr 26. UP. Alamosa, Colo. Amateur displayed colored movie of something in the sky.

Apr 27. AP. Washington, D.C. The Air Force announced that they "are not a joke".

Apr 27. AP. Chicago. Reported by pilot.

Apr 27. UP sent out the same story with a Kansas City dateline.

Apr 27. Seattle *Post-Intelligencer*. Local viewer, not picked up. The guy was only a salesman.

Apr 27. *Oregonian* editorialized.

Apr 28. AP. Grants Pass, Oregon. Reported by airport personnel.

Apr 29. UP. San Bruno, Calif. Reported by police.

Apr 29. UP. Centralia, Wash. Local viewer.

Apr 29. UP. Seattle. Local viewers.

Apr 30. Sioux City, Ia., *Journal*. Air stewardess reported one over South Bend, Ind. Not picked up.

May 4. Oakland, Calif., *Post-Enquirer*, feature story on p. 1, by Janet Henderson, local inventor as of 1912.

May 4. Buffalo *Courier-Express* columnist Rollin Palmer, again. His corresp sent him translation from *La Hora*, Quito, Ecuador. Story of a landing at Lardeo, Texas, April 16. Other details as in Dimmick above.

May 4. Reuters. Trieste. A photo taken April 14.

May 5. Billy Rose got into the act in his syndicated col.

May 6. AP. Rome, Italy. Local viewers.

May 13. UP. London. An explanation as printed in *News Review*, a mag.

May 14. AP. Minneapolis. The local *Tribune* conducted a poll on the subject.

May 16. St. Louis *Post-Dispatch*. Local viewer, not picked up.

May 16. UP. Savannah, Ga. Eddie Rickenbacker got in the act.

May 21. UP. Montrose, Calif. Local viewer.

May 22. *Wyoming State Tribune*. Reported by six National Guard pilots.

May 22. AP. Flagstaff, Ariz. A Lowell Observatory astronomer presented the local paper with a written statement that he had seen one. Seymour L. Hess, by name.

May 24. Special to the Denver *Post* from Montrose, Calif. Local viewers, not picked up.

May 25. AP. New York. Fawcett publisher of Keyhoe announced book by Keyhoe, asserting that "the government had protested the publication" of it. Copies were recalled from stands.

May 25. Weston County (Wyo.) *Gazette*. Local viewers, not picked up.

May 30. UP. Washington, D.C. Reported by a pilot.

June *True Magazine*, prints a despatch from Lowell Harmer, out of Mexico City, March 27. Cities local viewers. Ed ties story to a Senator from New Mexico.

June 6. AP. South Boston. Local viewer.

June 7. *Daily Express*, England. Reported by an RAF jet pilot.

June 7. Pittsburgh *Sun-Telegraph*. Wilkinsburg police found something.

June 8. *New Chronicle, England*. "A Cwmbran engineer" saw, "over Llantarnam (Monmouthshire)." Also in *Herald*, and in *Express*. No pick up in USA.

June 8. The *Telephone Register* of McMinnville, Oregon, printed a photo taken by a local. So many orders for that issue were received they reprinted the page.

June 9. Special to the Buffalo *News* from Dunkirk, N.Y. Local viewers, no pick up.

June 11. The *Oregonian* reprinted the McMinnville photo too. Later INP sent it to their papers, thoroughly retouched. AP and Reuters picked it up

Jnue 12. AP. Indianapolis. Rickenbacker cracks again.

June 13. Boston *Globe*. Feature "guess" by Joseph F. Dinneen.

June 13. *Daily Herald*, England. Explanation by

Stanley Bishop. UP picked it up in USA.

June 14. *Pathfinder.* Report of a pilot, and publicity for Keyhoe's book which was back on the stands. Surprised?

June 17. Oakland *Tribune.* Local viewers, no pick up. They were painters.

June 21. Roanoke, Va., *News.* Local viewer, not picked up.

June 22. AP. Oakland. Three United States Air Force non-coms reported one to the *Tribune,* so AP picked it up. So did INS. It was printed around the world.

June 23. Keene (?) *Sentinel.* Local viewer, no pick up.

June 24. *Oregonian.* Explanation.

June 24. AP. Dallas. Called a "meteor", but "saucer" worked into the story.

June 26. *Life,* a mag, printed the McMinnville photos.

June 27. Los Angeles *Herald-Express.* Reported by airliner crew. Seen 24th over southern Idaho.

June 28. UP picked it up.

June 29. UP. Phoenix, Ariz. Weather bureau and airline crew reported.

June 29. *Rockbridge County News,* Lexington, Va. Local viewer, no pick up.

June 30(?). *Arizona Republic.* A preacher, former pilot, reported one over Kingman, Kans.

June 30. *Arizona Republic.* Local viewers, no pick up.

June 30. D. C. *Times-Herald.* Local viewer, no pick up.

July *Reader's Digest.* Condensed from radio broadcast of Henry J. Taylor.

July 3. INS. Anchorage, Alaska. The commanding general of the armed forces in Alaska reported it. AP picked it up next day.

July 5. Hamilton (Ont.) *Spectator.* Local viewer, no pick up.

July 5. Detroit *News.* Local viewers, no pick up.

July 6. UP. Dowagiac, Mich. Farmer reported that he saw an Air Force C-54 launch a saucer whilst flying.

July 6. UP. Washington, D.C. The Air Force said he was mistaken.

July 6. AP. Los Angeles. A former marine corps aerial photographer reported.

July 9. In his column in the *Her-Trib,* John J. O'Neill suggested forming Saucer Clubs. (The woods is now full of them.)

July 9. San Francisco *Chronicle* ran a resume of the year's sightings.

July 11. *Herald News* (?New Jersey?) Letter from reader and an editorial.

July 12. UP. Memphis. Reported to the Navy by two pilots and an electronics instructor—seen on a radar screen.

July 12. Oakland *Tribune.* In Martinez, Calif. Advertising scheme or joke.

July 15. INS. Fort Monmouth, N.J. Local viewers.

July 15. W. W. Baker in the Kansas City *Star* wrote about Fort. The piece was widely reprinted.

July 18. Chehalis, Wash., *Chronicle.* Local viewers, no pick up.

July 20. UP. Seattle. Army intelligence at Fort Lewis reported.

July 26. Los Angeles *Times.* Local viewers, no pick up.

July 31. Edmonton (Alberta) *Bulletin.* Local viewers, no pick up.

Aug 7. Moline (Ill.) *Dispatch.* Local viewers, no pick up.

Aug 12. UP. Portland, Oregon. Reported by city firemen.

Aug 16. Los Angeles *Mirror.* Local viewers, no pick up.

Aug 22. Moline (Ill.) *Dispatch.* Reported by officials of the airport, but not picked up.

Sept. 11. AP. Mitchell Air Force Base, N.Y. Reported by a jet pilot.

Sept 19. UP. Poplar Bluff, Mo. Civil Aeronautics Authority and National Guard reported. It was printed as far away as Glasgow (Scotland).

Sept 27. AP. Philadelphia. Police reported.

Oct 1. New York *Times.* Publicity on the Scully book.

Oct 5. AP. Great Falls, Montana. Color film taken Aug 15 now turned over to Air Force.

Oct 6. Denver *Post.* Reported by pilots.

Oct 7. Roanoke, Va. *World News.* Local viewer, not picked up.

Oct 8. *Rocky Mountain News* printed a coupon asking readers to report anything they saw, and asking—"Do you really believe there are such things as flying fireballs, spaceships, flying saucers, etc.?"

Oct 11. INS. Chicago. Sighting, but called a meteor.

Oct 16. London *Times,* quotes the Astronomer Royal.

Oct 20. UP. Denver. "Geophysicist Silas M. Newton . . . told a Denver U class recently that four saucers had crashed and had been studied by the US govt. Bodies of 34 men, from 38 to 42 inches tall, were found in the wreckage, he said."

If this is the same bloke and the same speech mentioned above, read on. YS cannot say from the evidence whether this is a new "expert" or the same one.

Oct 22. AP. Berlin, Germany, printed in the *Telegraf.* Local viewers in "middle" France.

Oct 22. Manchester *Guardian.* Reported by locals in Lincolnshire. Not picked up in USA.

Oct 23. *N. N. Mail, England.* Reported over Edinburgh.

Oct 23. Paris edn of the N. Y. *Her-Trib.* UP. London. A man has built a model for the Festival.

Oct 24. *Daily Mirror,* London. An inquiry from a reader.

Oct 24. *Sunday Express,* London. A pilot reports seeing something in 1931.

Oct 26. *Daily Herald,* England. Local viewer, no pick up.

Oct. Gerald Heard published his book, *Is Another World Watching?* Some of it appeared serially in the *Express.*

November. The *Good News Broadcaster,* official organ of the Back to the Bible Broadcast, Lincoln, Neb., prints a piece on our subject by R. S. Beal, Pastor of First Baptist Church, Tucson, Ariz. It says no more and no less than any other "expert" pronunciamento on the subject.

Nov 1. *N. N. Mail,* England. Reported by Paignton (Devon) police.

Nov 6. Manchester *Guardian*. London sighting is spoofed.

Nov 7. Liverpool *Echo*. Report in Southport, not picked up.

Nov 9. Oakland *Tribune*. Reported by police and fiermen.

Nov 11. Reuters. Rio de Janeiro, Brazil. Reported at Caruari.

Harold E. Watson, intelligence chief at Wright Field's Air Command, as "the air force's foremost authority".

Nov 12. INS staffman Bob Considine, quotes Col. (Wright Field is at Dayton, Ohio.)

Nov 12. *Sunday Dispatch*, England. Reported by airmen, over London.

Nov. 13. "TP" in the Pittsburgh *Daily Reporter*. Santiago, Chile. Reported by "members of the diplomatic corps".

Nov 14. Liverpool *Echo*. Reported by Crewe police. police.

Nov 15. INS staffman Bob Considine tries very hard to "debunk" the whole business. See the Cincinnati *Enquirer* of this date.

Nov 16. Philadephia *Inquirer*, special from Reading. Reported by a radio control operator.

Nov 19. Pittsburgh *Sun-Telegraph*. Local viewers, not picked up.

Nov. 19. *Sunday Disptach, England*. Reported by a Wing-Commander.

Nov 21. *Evening Chronicle*, Newcastle, Eng. Debunking article by Frank J. Acfield.

Nov 24. Liverpool *Echo*. Local doctor of Rhyl, no pick up.

Nov 26. *Sunday Dispatch*, England, printed a resume of public opinion on the subject.

Nov 28. AP. Huron, S.D. Reported by the weather bureau.

Dec 2. Ellenton, S. C. Direct quote of first sentence. "Were flying saucers spying on the proposed site of the nation's first hydrogen bomb plant Friday night?"

Will some member please tell me why I'm wasting my time on this nonsense? The pattern is perfectly clear. From this point on, the digest will simply state where the word "saucer" occurred in the "news".

Dec 3. *Empire News*, Eng.

Dec 3. *Sunday Dispatch*, Eng.

Dec 4. *Daily Herald*, Eng.

Dec 4. *N. N. Mail*, Eng.

Dec 4. Iowa City *Times*.

Dec 6. Manchester *Guardian*.

Dec 6. *Daily Express*, Eng.

Dec 8. *Daily Herald*, Eng.

Dec 20. *Daily Express*, Eng.

Dec 25. AP, Honolulu.

Dec 29. Syndicated column of Robert C. Ruark, humorist.

## 1951 = 21 FS

Jan 2. *Daily Mail*, Eng.

Jan 5. San Francisco *Examiner*, "by law enforcement officers".

Jan 12. *News Chronicle*, London. At Birmingham.

Jan 21. AP. Kansas City, Mo., "by a veteran pilot."

Jan 26. AP. Stockholm, "by Swedish defense staff."

Jan 29. UP. Same story. Perhaps member dated clipping wrongly.

Feb 26. *Newsweek*.

Feb 28. Los Angeles *Times*.

Apr 4. AP. New York. *Life* mag is cited and quoted.

May 23. UP. Reports from Kansas and Minnesota.

May 23. Toronto *Telegram*, "Ontario, Kansas and Minnesota."

July 23. Hollywood *Citizen-News*. Reported in Tujunga.

July 27. New Brighton, Pa., *News-Tribune*.

Aug 1. AP. Youngstown, Ohio.

Aug. 2. AP. Hagerstown, Md.

Aug 26. AP and UP. Lubbock, Texas. Reported by profs of Texas Tech.

Sept 11. UP. Mitchell Field, N. Y. Two Air Force jet pilots reported chasing something.

Sept 11. Letter from Camp Stoneman. See letters from Members division.

Sept 20. AP's Blakeslee.

Sept. *See*, a mag. Article by the Britisher, Heard.

Oct 10. Hamilton (Ont) *Spectator*.

Oct 12. Air Force "warning" printed in *Newsday*, Long Island.

Oct 25. *Press-Citizen*, Iowa City, Ia.

Oct 27. San Bernardino *Daily Sun*.

Nov 5. Glendale (Calif) *News-Press*. Seen by the reporter himself, Thomas Weeles.

Nov 9. AP. Albuquerque, N.M. *La Paz* roars again.

Nov 9. N. Y. *Journal-American*.

Nov 16. Liverpool *Echo* quotes pilot in Hong Kong. Also in *Daily Mail*. Picked up by AP.

Nov 22. Acme Telephoto of one, Riverside, Calif.

Dec 3. Hamilton (Ont) *Spectator*.

## 1952 = 22 FS

Jan 7. MFS Meade Layne who runs BSRA, in advertising a booklet of his, states: "One short interview with a Disc-occupant has taken place."

Jan 17. Reuters, Melbourne, Australia.

Jan. Ray Palmer, the ed of several Chicago and vicinity mags of sensationalism, one time sponsor of Shaver and his underground folk, announced publication of a book written by Ken Arnold and himself. Arnold had been after YS to have the Society sponsor him on a lecture tour before that.

Feb 6. El Paso *Herald-Post*. Also *Times*, same city.

Feb. *Progressive World*, p. 99.

Feb 19. UP. Washington, D.C. Air Force announced sighting by bomber crews in Korea.

Feb. 18. N. Y. *Her Tribune* printed col by Joseph and Stewart Alsop, Washington (D.C.) dateline.

Feb 20. AP. Albuquerque. La Paz!

Feb 20. AP. Tokyo.

Feb 20. UP. Washington, D.C.

Feb 20. AP. White Sands reported.

Feb 27. *Oberlausitzer Rundschau*, Germany.

Mar 11. Amarillo (Texas) *Daily News*, printed letter from MFS Markham.

Mar 24. Letter in *Time*, a mag.

Mar 25. Boston *Trav*. Col by Bill Schofield.

Mar 27. *Bulletin*, Grants Pass, Oregon, again.

Apr 3. AP. Tucson, Ariz.

Apr 3. UP. Benson, Ariz., same story. "Two Air Force pilots . . . "

Apr 4. AP. New York *Life*, a mag, quizzed Air Force.

Apr 4. AP. Washington, D.C. Air Force replied.

Apr 10. Toronto *Globe and Mail*, an anonymous astronomer saw something two years ago. Photo of this coot, hiding half his face with a mag. The Journal of the Royal Astronomical Society of Canada is cited: Nov. 1913, "luminous bodies in formation over US and Bermuda:" Inverness, Scotland, 1848: Venice and France, 1877.

Apr 11. UP. Minneapolis. "Experts" of General Mills, saw "last October". They want 24-hour sky watch instituted.

Apr 12. N. Y. *Times* editorialized, mentioning Fort.

Apr 12. AP. Washington, D.C. Pronouncement from the Air Force. Sighting in Arizona.

Apr 14, papers were still printing the story of Apr 11, about the General Mills "experts".

Apr 14. Reported seen at "Sandia"—no State indicated.

Apr 15. AP. Winchester, Va.

Apr 16. CP. North Bay, Ont. Reported by RCAF officials. Seen over "vital jet base".

Apr 17. Edmonton (Alberta) *Journal*, editorial.

Apr 18. INS. Las Vegas, Nevada. Air Force officer saw "over or very close to test site, where important new atomic tests are in progress."

Apr 19. Alton (Ill.) *Evening Telegraph* editorialized.

Apr 19. Toronto *Telegram*. Pronouncement of Dominion Astronomer, Dr. Peter M. Millman.

Apr 21. CP. Ottawa, Can. Caandian Air Force pronouncement.

Apr 23. CP. Winnepeg. Observed at Molson, Man.

Apr 25. Calgary *Herald*.

Apr 27. Bluefield, W. Va. *Daily Telegraph*. Editorial.

Apr 27. N. Y. *Times* Book Review Section quotes Heard book.

Apr 29. *Deseret News*, Salt Lake City. Seen in Utah.

Apr 30. Seattle *Post-Intelligencer*. Something seen.

May 5. *N. N. Mail*. Seen in New South Wales. B.U.P.

May 5. Ottawa *Journal*. "Second in five days."

May 6. UP. Durango, Colo. "Over uranium plant".

May 6. *Daily Express*, Eng. Over Sydney, Australia.

May 7. Columnist Paul Light in the St. Paul *Pioneer Press*, mentions man who saw one 60 years ago. Two weeks later, May 21, Light used same copy verbatim.

May 9. Newcastle *Chronicle*. Photos taken near Rio to be sent to Air Force, Washington. Also in Manchester *Guardian*.

May 9. MFS Markham has another letter in the Amarillo *News*.

May 11. San Francisco *Examiner*. Local sighting.

May 12. UP. Seattle. Although called a "meteor blast", "saucers" was worked into the first paragraph.

May 13. N. Y. *Times* editorial spoofing at the "prosaic" explanation of the Seattle blast.

May 13. *N. N. Mail*, Eng. Over French Morocco.

May 14. Ottawa *Journal*. Letter on *Revelations*.

May 19. Manchester *Guardian* editorial.

May 20. *Ibid*. Britain's hum linked to "saucers".

May 21. *Northrop News*, organ of Northrop Aircraft Inc., Hawthorne, Calif. Leo Swenson saw. Illust.

May 22. AP. Chicago. One chased an airliner.

May 25. *Sunday Dispatch*, Eng., published the Brazilian photos mentioned above.

May 26. AP. Tyler, Texas. Local sighting.

May 27. *N. N. Mail*, Eng. French savant scoffs.

May 30. Liverpool *Echo*. Local sighting.

May, about. Mimeo sheet from David Gordon. Explanation.

May. MFS Meade Layne got out another something or other, utterly incomprehensible, but containing comments by a name we like. It is—spelled just this way—YADaDI SHITTE.

May 30. CP. Vancouver. By a pilot.

June 1. *Sunday Disptach*, Eng. Seen in Southern England.

June 4. *Daily Mail*, Eng. B.U.P. says Dr. Menzel of Harvard can make saucer effects in his kitchen.

June 10. Same story but longer in Denver *Post*.

June 11. *Variety* gives low-down on Menzel and rivalry of *Life* versus *Look*. See *Look* June 17 and *Life* June 9.

June 11. Denver *Post*. Local sighting

June 11. MFS Mitchell saw something on Long Island.

June 11. *Morning Avalanche*, Lubbock, Texas. Quotes *Time*, *Life*, *Look*.

June 16. HFFS Russell got a letter pubd in *Life*, international edition, not USA.

June 16. AP. Richmond, Va. Something seen. Also an explanation in a letter from Milwaukee, Wis.

June 17. INS. Paris. By operators of an airport. In Manchester *Guardian* two days later

June 17. Manchester *Guardian* editorial.

June 17. UP. New York. Exploits *Look* article.

June 18. UP. Pueblo, Colo. By local weather bureau.

June 18. *People Today*, a mag. Seen in Los Angeles.

June 19. Pittsburgh *Post*. Seen in New South Wales and Victoria, Australia.

June 20. St. Louis *Globe-Democrat*. Two observers.

June 21. AP. Richmond, Va. Local sightings.

June 21. AP. Washington, D.C. Local sightings.

June 22. Amarillo, Texas, has a "Sighting Center", as in Los Angeles. *News-Globe*.

June 23. UP. Middlton, Pa. Air Force reported "over Jersey shore"

June 29. Atlanta *Journal*. Local sighting.

June 30. Denver *Post*. Local sightings.

June. NANA, Berlin. A confused piece about a "landing" and a crew of two members, seen in an East German forest. Author Antony Terry asks—"are they a Russian invention?"

July 2. *Daily Express*, Eng. A resume, with explanations.

July 3. CP. Ajax, Ont. Local sighting.

July 4. UP. Chicago. Reported by Air Force officers.

July 4. Meridional News Agency. Taken from a news broadcast. That a photo had been taken near Belo Horizonte, Minas Geraes State, South America. *Cr* Kuhn (translation).

July 5. Chicago *Daily News* printed the blast of the Paris prof, issued May 27.

July 5. UP. Denver. Four veteran pilots reported,

seen in Washington State, "hovering over an atomic plant".

July 7. Denver *Post.* Two more sightings, local.

July 7. UP. Los Angeles. A Royal Air Force officer arrived from White Sands and announced that what he had been told in White Sands made him "believe" in them.

July 7. Ogden, Utah, *Standard-Examiner.* "Probably a meteor" but "saucers" mentioned.

July 8. Pittsburgh *Press.* Something seen.

July 10. *Realtor News,* Lancaster, Calif. Reprinted from *The Desert Wings.* Sightings.

July 14. Ottawa, Ill., *Republican-Times.* Local sighting.

July 14. Peoria, Ill., *Star.* Local sighting.

July 14. Manchester *Guardian.* Sighting at Hereford.

July 15. Los Angeles *Times.* Reports a meeting of "Civilian Saucer Investigation". Also Western Air Defense Force has an alleged 6000 watchers at it.

July 15. UP. Miami, Fla. Sighting by pilots near Norfolk, Va.

July 15. *Deseret News,* Salt Lake City. Local sighting.

July 15. Ogden, Utah, *Standard-Examiner.* Local sighting.

July 15. UP. Boise, Idaho. Local sighting.

July 16. Peoria *Star.* Gomer Bath col.

July 16. UP. Washington, D.C. The Air Force announced that it was investigating the sighting near Norfolk.

July 16. *Oregonian.* Portland sighting explained.

July 16. AP dug up locals at Norfolk who also saw.

July 17. Dayton, O., *Journal-Herald.* Local sighting with diagram.

July 17. AP. "Tidewater Virginians" saw something.

July 17. Miami *Herald.* Locals saw something "two months ago".

July 17. AP. Yreka, Calif. Sighting.

July 18. Dunedin *Evening Star.* The US Air Force announced it had received 60 reports in the past two weeks. Same story by UP, Dayton, Ohio, dateline.

July 18. INS. Chicago. Pilot saw near Denver.

July 18. Hartford *Times* states that Air Force "admits" people see things, because their boys see things on radar.

July 18. AP. Washington, D.C. Radio engineer saw.

July 19. Keene *Eve. Sentinel.* Jest of the ed.

July 20. Roanoke, Va. *Times.* Local sighting.

July 21. Pittsburgh *Sun Teleg.* Local sighting.

July 20. Chicago *Trib* Press Service, Washington, D.C. The Air Force announced what people on the West Coast would see.

July 21. Peoria *Star.* Gomer Bath col. Another, July 22.

July 21. AP. Washington, D.C. "The Air Force said today . . . " etc. New sightings alleged at Burlington, Vt., South Portland, Me., Staten Island, N. Y.

July 21. AP. Dallas. Sighting by pilot.

July 20 or 22. Santa Fe *New Meixcan.* UP. Sightings at Albuquerque, Portale and vicitiny.

July 22. AP. Washington. Air Force announcement about sightings on radar near D.C.

July 22. Chicago *Trib* Press Service. Reporter asked attache of Russian Embassy, Washington, if saucers came from Russia. He said no.

July 22. Dayton O., *Journal-Herald.* Letter from Culver City. Humorous explanation.

July 22. AP. River Edge, N.J. An AP reporter, Saul Pett, writes that he saw.

July 22. In the Amarillo *Daily News,* one Robert S. Allen writing under a Chicago dateline, mixes up anti-Russ charges, saucers and La Paz.

July 22. AP. Strasburg, Va. It was a weather balloon.

July 23. San Francisco *Call.* Sighting at Santa Cruz, Calif.

July 23. Roanoke, Va. *Times.* Local sightings.

July 23. Amarillo *Daily News.* Sighting at Portales.

July 23. Peoria *Star.* Gomer Bath col.

July 23. AP. Boston. Coast Guard reports.

July 23. Dunedin *Eve Star.* Sighting over Hamilton.

July 23. UP. Washington. Air Force denied 24-hour watch by Civilian Ground Observer Corps was to look for saucers or *vice versa.*

July 24. AP. Columbus, O. Six armed jets chased something they could not catch.

July 24. Roanoke, Va. *Times.* Local sighting.

July 24. Letter in the Sacramento *Bee* says saucers are waste of space in papers.

July 24. Pittsburgh *Post-Gazette.* Local sighting.

July 24. Dallas *Morning News.* Sighting and explanation.

July 24. Whitney Bolton Syndicated column.

July 26. AP. Titusville, Pa. Sighting.

July 28. AP. Washington. "The Air Force said—no emergency". Jets in Washington had chased radar blips. No catchum.

July 28. Los Angeles *Times.* Local sighting with drawing. Sighting also in Indianapolis.

July 28. Liverpool *Echo.* Local sighting.

July 28. Drew Pearson syndicated col.

July 29. UP. Chicago. Rocketeer and MFS Farnsworth got into the papers telegraphing Truman and others not to shoot at saucers.

July 29. Seattle *Times.* A prof at U of Washington said the stuff about sightings was a comfort to "potential enemies".

July 29. Miami *Herald.* Local sightings.

July 29. Miami *Daily News* scare-headed INS story on Air Force frustration. Almost entire first page devoted to it.

July 29. Same technique employed by Newark, N. J. *Star Ledger* on its UP story.

July 29. N. Y. *Times* went the other way, even discounting radar.

July 29. Pittsburgh *Press* editorial suggests that "It's time the government quit playing jokes on the people".

July 29. London *Evening Standard.* Sightings in many quarters of France.

July. La Paz was also hot again.

July 29. St. Paul *Dispatch* played it big, also Los Anegles, Pittsburgh and Amarillo papers. Reward of $500 offered for a photo.

July 29. Pittsburgh *Post-Gazette.* Local sightings.

July 29. Sacramento. Local sightings.

July 29. Watson Davis. Director of Science Service wrote that government should tell the people what it knows.

July 29. Columnist Fred Othman wrote about Keyhoe.

July 30. Los Angeles *Herald* & *Express* ran headline: FLYING SAUCERS 6-HR RAID ON WASHINGTON.

July 29. San Francisco *Call-Bulletin*. Sighting reported by law enforcement officers.

July 30. Atlanta *Journal* took the negative side of the scare, but reported local sightings. Also quoted the Cleveland *Press*, recounting an "attack" by one in 1951 over Augusta, Ga.

July 30. AP. Enid, Okla. Local sighting.

July 30. Miami *Daily News* prints a night-time photo "released without comment" by the US Marines.

July 31. NEA sent out photos of the radar pips.

July 31. UP. Kalama, Wash. Plywood box of instruments fell.

July 29, 30, 31. INS Special story by Keyhoe, now called, "Washington representative of True Magazine."

July 30. Los Angeles *Herald and Express*. Local sightings.

July 30. Chicago. James T. Mangam, who claims to own all "space" forbid saucers to trespass.

July 30. Elizabeth, N. J. *Journal* editorial.

July 30. Liverpool *Echo* quotes *Daily Post* explanation.

July 31. INS. Washington, tells of radar false alarm in Alaska, May 11, 1943.

July 31. AP. Hot Springs, Ark. Local sightings.

July 31. NEA. Washington, by Douglas Larsen. Resume of recent phenom.

July 31. Atlanta *Journal* editorial, photo from Kutztown, Pa. (UP)

July 31. Albuquerque, N.M. Sighting by newsman.

Aug 1. Atlanta *Journal* prints a photo—day-time—released by the Coast Guard.

Aug 1. AP. Washington. Further, widespread use of Coast Guard photo from Salem, Mass.

Aug 1. Los Angeles papers, new sightings in Santa Monica, Pasadena, L. A., Indio.

Aug 1. Calgary *Albertan*, NEA photo, taken in Jersey City by a plane spotter.

Aug 1. Pittsburgh *Press*. Letter from reader.

Aug 2. AP. Champaign, Ill. A "river" showed on radar.

Aug 2. Liverpool *Echo*. That US Air Force said it had 432 written reports so far this year.

Aug 2. Pittsburgh *Post* editorial.

Aug 2. AP. Seoul. Sightings in Korea and Japan.

Aug 2. UP. Lancaster, Calif By deputy sheriffs.

Aug. 3. Pittsburgh *Sun-Telegraph*. Old fashioned puzzle run as "Operation Flying Saucer".

Aug 3. Roanoke, Va. *Times*. Explanation.

Aug 3. AP. Washington Maj. Gen. Roger M. Ramey, Air Force Saucerman went on TV.

Aug 3. CP. Montreal. Flash and explosion, like meteor, now mystery.

Aug 4. Los Angeles *Times*. "Flying saucers" photographed one mile down in ocean. Also, more local sightings in sky.

Aug 4. Columnist Thomas L. Stokes.

Aug 4. *Time*. On the radar in Washington.

Aug 4. Bluefield, W. Va. *Sunset News* editorial and cartoon.

Aug 4. *Life*. Washington's Blips.

Aug 4. Pittsburgh *Sun-Telegraph*. Sighting called "meteorite".

Aug 5. Pittsburgh *Press* quotes Dr. E. C. Crentz of Carnegie Tech Nuclear Research Center, "Maybe God is just trying to confuse us." Same paper, Perseids predicted.

Aug 5. Los Angeles *Times*. Air Force announced it had a form printed to be filled out by sighters.

Aug 5. AP. Washington. Semi-humorous feature by Frank Carey.

Aug 6. AP. Evansville, Ind. The rocks falling on Schattin house linked to saucers.

Aug 6. AP. Washington. Spokesman for Army Engineers, Noel Scott, showed how to make saucers in a vacuum jar.

Aug 6. San Francisco *Examiner*. Local sightings.

Aug 6. AP. Washington. New "invasion" on radar screen

Aug 6. AP. New York, feature by Relman Morin, quotes Charles Fort.

Aug 7. Manchester *Guardian* cites Munich monthly, *Flieger*, that a giant Russian flying saucer propelled by 46 jet engines recently crash-landed on Spitsbergen. British UP.

Aug 7. AP feature by Saul Pett. Reports set all-time high past week.

Aug 8. CP. Montreal. Follow-up on explosion a week before, still headlined "saucers".

Aug 8. *The Catholic Standard*, Washington, D. C., quotes the Very Rev. Francis J. Connell, C. SS. R., dean of School of Sacred Theology. Okays life "similar to ours" on other planets.

Aug 9. UP. Pittsburgh. Local sighting.

Aug 9. Chicago *Daily News* Service. Explanation by Arthur J. Snider.

Aug 10. Pittsburgh *Press* links Perseids to saucers.

Aug 11. *Life* printed the Coast Guard picture.

Aug 11. *Time* printed the Coast Guard picture.

Aug 11. Stroudsburg, Pa., *Record*, "not a saucer".

Aug 11. Seattle *Post-Intelligencer* reprints the one about a landing in East Germany, see above.

Aug 11. Glendale, Calif., *News-Press*. Letter suggests pilots are vegetables.

Aug 13. AP. Jerusalem. London *Jewish Chronicle* has "Haifa". Sighting.

Aug 14. AP, Tucson, Ariz. Reported by Reserve Air Force pilot.

Aug 16. AP. Washington. The father of radar speaks. Dr. Robert M. Page, that is

Aug 17. AP. Caracas, Venezuela. Sightings. British UP adds that jets were sent to intercept.

Aug 17. Pittsburgh *Press*. Local inventor.

Aug 17. *Humboldt Times*, Eureka, Calif. Firemen report.

Aug 18. *Time*, a mag. Quotes Father Connell on the religion of the saucers.

Aug 20. Liverpool *Echo*. Two photos, one by a Blackpool newsman.

Aug 21. AP. Washington. "The Air Force today released" the last message received from Capt. Thomas Mantell who died chasing something over Fort Knox, Ky., Jan 7. 1948.

Aug 23. AP. Mountain View, Calif. Veteran Navy flier reports.

Aug 23. Came DESVERGERS, the Scoutmaster

and former Marine. He and three boys about 11, saw something near West Palm Beach. It shot at him, etc. AP picked it up. Air Force sent officers to question him. Later he turned up with a publicity man whose name is very like that of a press agent YS knew in Hollywood some years ago.

Local members supplemented printed stories by personal investigations and interviews. The Scoutmaster has a local reputation for the vividness of his imagination.

The story went around the world, biggest thing since Keyhoe.

Aug 24. Pittsburgh *Press* Roto section, photos.

Aug 25. Stroudsburg, Pa. *Record.* Managing ed of Titusville *Herald* saw, he says.

Aug 25. Los Angeles *Evening Herald.* Letter from man who says saw one stand still over Los Alamos for an hour and a half. Where were the jets? Another letter, sighting Aug 3.

Aug 26. Peoria *Star,* Gomer Bath col. Same on Aug 27, and 29.

Aug 27. INS. St. Louis. Astronomer says, "all imagination".

Aug 28. AP. West Palm Beach. Other sightings nine or ten hours after Desvergers.

Aug 29. INS. Reading, Pa. Airport employe saw one released by a jet in midair.

Aug 30. AP. Honolulu. Hawaiians have known about them for a thousand years.

Sept 1. Reuters, Kyoto, Japan. Reported by firemen. AP picked it up, also INS.

Sept 2. *Sunday Times,* Eng. Pitreavie, Fife. RAF studying sightings.

Sept 2. Los Angeles *Times.* Local sightings.

Sept 3. Los Angeles *Mirror.* Different ones.

Sept 6. UP picked up the Pittsburgh inventor above.

Sept 7. AP. Rome, quotes local "Communist" paper. Visiting astronomer says no sightings over Russia.

Sept 12. Meridional News Agency, from a radio broadcast. Sighting at Belem, Macapa—Amapa Territory, South America. *Cr.* Kuhn (Translation).

Sept 13. Bluefield, W. Va., *Sunset News.* Local sightings.

Sept 13. AP. Baltimore Sightings—"East Coast area states".

Sept 13. Pittsburgh *Press.* photo weather balloon.

Sept 13. AP. London, Eng. British Interplanetary Society scoffs.

Sept 14. AP. UP, INS, Sutton, W. Va. Housewife and six boys including one aged 17 who is a National Guardsman, were looking for a spot where one was supposed to have landed. There they say they saw a monster.

Sept 14. AP. Copenhagen. Reported by an officer of the Danish Navy.

Sept 15. *Time,* a mag. A Swendenborgian writes on the theology of saucers.

Sept 15. AP. Geneva, Switzerland. A magician at their International Congress caused saucers to fly.

Sept 16. UP. Myrtle Beach, S. C. Local sighting.

Sept 17. Miami *Daily News.* Sighting at Belle Glade, Fla.

Sept 18. Philadelphia *Inquirer.* Local sighting near Naval base.

Sept 19. Edmondton (Alberta) *Journal.* Local sighting.

Sept 20. Liverpool *Echo.* Sighting by RAF men over Topcliffe, Yorks. Also in *Evening Standard,* etc.

Sept 21. Reuters quotes that Robert S. Allen man, in the N. Y. *Post,* as writing that "the Kremlin had four different investigations under way to discover their identity and sources".

Sept 23 (?). Indianapolis *Star.* Rome, an astronomer "caught" one in his telescope, scoffed.

Sept 27. *N. N. Mail.* Near Florence, Italy, one hovered, and fired a "ray gun" at a fisherman.

Sept 27. *Star Weekly,* Toronto, reprinted a resume from *US NEWS & World Report.*

Sept 29. Hamburg, Germany, Kolner *Stadt-Anzeiger.* Sightings in North Germany, Denmark and Southern Sweden. *Cr* Mitchell (Translation) Also in *Die Welt.*

Sept 30. *Evening Star,* Eng. Sighting in Otahuhu, Austrialia.

Oct 2. New York "scientist" went to Sutton, W. Va. Found nothing. Princeton, W. Va. *Observer.*

Oct 4. AP. Balboa, Calif. Sighting at sea.

Oct 7. AP. Goteborg, Sweden. Photo—"of Jupiter".

Oct 9. DPA, Stockholm, Sweden. Germans tried saucers in 1944. *Cr* Mitchell, (translation).

Oct 10. Albany, N. Y. *Knickerbocker News.* Blast in sky.

Oct 13. AP. Wellington, New Zealand. "Scientists" form saucer club.

Oct 15. Denver dateline, in the Pittsburgh *Press.* Silas M. Newton—see above for his speech to the U of Denver "science" class, was charged with swindling a Denver businessman out of $50,000, Accto *Saturday Review,* one Leo a. GeBauer is co-defendent, and at last accounts they both were missing.

Scully relied heavily upon these two for "evidence" in his book.

Oct 18. Dallas, *Morning News.* Local sightings. Also seen in Louisiana.

Oct 19. AP. Tokyo. Sightings in Korea.

Oct 20. *Newsday.* Those blasts noted in earlier DOUBT attributed to "collision" of saucers.

Oct 20. Pittsburgh *Post-Gazette.* Local sighting.

Oct 25. Reuters, Bonn, Germany. Seen 70 years ago.

Oct 26. AP. Papeete, Tahiti. Known to Polynesians since "most ancient times".

Oct 26. AP. Aukland, New Zealand. Sighting.

Oct 29. French New Agency. Sighting over Gaillac, near Toulouse.

Oct 30. N. Y. *Journal-American.* Sighting by South American pilot.

Nov 23. *Sunday Dispatch,* Eng. Sighting on English coast, Sussex etc.

Nov 9. Galgary *Albertan.* Sighting at Wetaskiwin.

Nov 25. Los Angeles *Mirror.* Deputy sheriff sights again.

Nov 26. Near Sao Paulo, Brazil. Sighting by MFS Kuhn.

Nov 28. Edmonton (Alberta) *Journal.* Sighting.

Dec 4. *Antelope Valley Ledger-Gazette,* (?Calif?) Sighting.

Dec 9. New Haven, Conn., *Register.* Sighting at Derby.

Dec 10. AP. Washington. Explanation by Civil Aeronautics Administration of radar blips.

Dec 11. Santa Barbara, Calif., *News-Press.* Saucer Club recruiting "again".

Dec 15. AP. Charlottesville, Va. Sighting by airport manager.

Dec 19. CP. Prince Rupert, B. C. Sighting.

Dec 19. Edmonton (Alberta) *Journal.* Sighting at Leduc.

Dec 19. AP. Washington. Explanation in *Science Magazine.*

Dec 20. Flin Flon, Alberta. Local sighting.

Dec 21. Drew Pearson column. Sighting in Panama Canal Zone "for five hours and 36 minutes" on Nov 25.

## 1953 = 23 FS

Jan *Mechanix Illustrated,* a mag, shows a "Flying Saucer" camera.

Jan 6. UP. Dallas. Sighting.

Jan 9. UP. Santa Fe, N. M. White Sands is going to explain everything.

Jan 9. AP. Kerrville, Texas. Blame radio interference on one.

Jan 12. AP. Baldwyn, Miss. Sighting.

Jan 12. Dallas *News.* More seen.

Jan 21. AP. US Air Base, Northern Japan. Sightings. Chased by jets.

Jan 22. Chicago *Tribune* Press Service. Attributes sightings in Japan to Russian guided missiles.

Jan 27. AP. Tokyo. "The Air Force tonight reported a small metallic disc-shaped object made a controlled, sweeping pass at an American jet." Now it comes out that these sightings and this "pass" occurred March 29, 1952.

Jan 29. Los Angeles *Mirror.* Local sighting. Chased by jet.

Jan 30. Headlines on it.

Jan 31. Story denied.

Feb 3. Columnist Robert S. Allen quotes La Paz. That's a combination!

Feb 3. Columnist Matt Weinstock casts suspicion on the Air Force story by quoting an anonymous pilot who "was there" in March '52, and heard nothing of it, and knew no pilot of that name. Weinstock would be on firmer ground if he could name *his* man.

Feb 4. Toronto *Telegram.* Local sighting.

THAT IS ALL

Besides those data, properly labelled, we have a few which lack dates, place, or some other detail.

A letter and a funny picture from J. Pasqual Tump, Los Angeles.

From the October (?year?) *Irish Digest,* a sighting over County Wicklow in 1898. Liam Riordan in the *Irish Catholic.*

UP. New York. No date. Sightings over Staten Island, Massena, Oneida, N. Y.

UP. Pasco, Wash. Two newspaper editors sighted one "over Atomic Plant City".

INS. Dover, Del. Two Air Force pilots reported. No date.

Aug 16, 1951. No paper named. "South Fork" is something people fish in, wherever this came from.

Apr 10, 1592. A paper called *The Messenger* editorialized, but no city or State is indicated.

British UP, undated. Sightings in Montgomery, Ala., and Sioux City, Ia.

AP. No date, no source. Sighting at El Paso, Fort Worth, Galveston, Texas, Montgomery, Ala., Natchez, Miss.

Chicago *Daily News* Service. No date. Quotes astronomers as saying, funny, no astronomer ever saw a saucer.

Besides all the above, we have a good many letters from members who have observed objects in the sky through this period. They will be listed, perhaps printed, as space becomes available.

## NOTE

Photostats of the data above will be supplied at the rate of $1 per exposure. Small clippings can be fitted, several to one negative. Larger clippings will require two or three shots to get all in and be readable. Send your dollar with your order.

## METEORS

Concurrently with the long series of accounts employing the word "saucer", other stories of lights in the sky appeared without that word. The papers used "meteors" or "fireballs" to describe these others, and all too frequently mis-used the term "meteorite" for something seen in the air. Tell your reporter friends that a meteor does not become a meteorite until it is on the ground.

Oct 3, 1948, over South Head, Wick, England.

Oct 12, over Beadnell, Northumbria, England.

Oct 14. Southwest USA.

Dec 10, over Montreal and points in Maine.

Jan 16, 1949. Pruett on comets.

Jan 17, over Paris, Ky.

Jan 23, Pruett

Jan 28, over Seattle.

Jan 28, over Western France.

Jan 30, Pruett

Feb 8. Phoenix, Ariz. Order issued forbidding removal of meteorites from parks.

Feb 10, over Victoria, B. C.

Feb 13, Pruett

Apr 5, over Salt Lake City.

Apr 11, over Boston and New England generally. Seen by MFS Small, Providence, R. I.

Apr 11, over Newcastle, Del.

Jun 5, over entire State of Florida.

Sept 6, southeast coast of England, Folkstone, etc.

Sept 23, over Casper, Wyo.

Sept 23, in Caernarvonshire, a five pound meteorite set fire to the Prince Llewellen Hotel, at Beddgelert. Came through the roof.

Oct 13, over Buffalo and Toronto, aurora and meteor.

Oct 16, over Gaillac, France.

Oct 24, over Fort Williams, Ont.

Oct 28, over Buffalo and vicinity.

Nov 2. (Wed. before) over Waterloo, N. Y.

Dec 17, Centerville, Ia., stampeded cattle.

Jan 9, 1950, over Berwick, Yorks.

Jan 9, near New London, Conn.

July 4, (Sat. before) over Fairbanks, Alaska.

July 13, over Los Angeles.

Aug 11, Northwest USA.

Aug 19, over Seattle.

Sept 9, Pruett wants pieces.

Sept 15, (Thurs. before) over Central Calif.

Sept 20, exploded over Memphis which is jarred.

Sept 25, at Madisonville, Ky. Stone meteorite fell into backyard at Murray.

Oct 1, over Berwick, Yorks. Fell into sea, but called a "comet".

Oct 5, over Southern Wisconsin.

Oct 5, probably same one, seen Tennessee to Indiana.

Nov 3, Ottawa and Northeastern US.

Nov 7, over Western Oklahoma and Northern Texas.

Dec 4, (Sat. before) over North of England.

Dec 8, (Wed. before) over New England.

Dec 18, over New Mexico, (Sat. before).

Mar 7, 1951, over New Mexico. La Paz hot on trail!

May 11, over Melbourne, Australia. Exploded. Earth trembled three minutes.

Jul 8, over Detroit, (Sat. before). Seen also in Ohio.

Jul 12, denial was a meteor. Said was new type of plane light.

Aug 3, slow one over Pittsburgh.

Sept 26, struck ground in Southern Chile.

Oct 15, over Akron to Pittsburgh. Said to have been seen to burn itself out, 100 miles at sea off Pulaski, Va.

Nov 3, over five Southwestern States.

Nov 5, over Melbourne, Australia.

Nov 7, over Oklahoma and Texas.

Nov 8, over Arizona, and a different one over Texas.

Nov 8, La Paz has counted seven meteors in the S W in eleven days, called a record.

Nov 9, over Middleton, N. Y.

Nov 9, over Los Angeles, to the North.

Nov 9, two more, one in Texas, one in Mexico. La Paz makes the score 8 in 13 days, as of Nov 10.

Nov 12, over Buffalo.

Nov 14, over El Paso, Texas.

Nov 16, over Sonoma, Calif.

Nov 21, over N. M.

Nov 23, over Puerto Rico

Nov 27, over Hobbs, N. M.

Dec 1, over Arizona.

Dec 16, Pruett is miffed at La Paz for stealing the green-fire show.

Jan 2, 1952. AP quoted La Paz—the meteors "could be" guided missiles.

Jan 2, over Dublin, Ireland.

Jan 4, over Madera, Calif.

Jan 10, over Vancouver, B. C.

Jan 12, the Chicago Herald-American today got around to printing the AP despatch that appeared in most papers Nov 9.

Jan 28, over Northwest England.

Jan 29, near Elmira, N. Y.

Feb 1, over Oklahoma.

Feb 10, *Parade* worked "saucers" into a resume of La Paz. Sorry. This belongs in the other column.

Feb 14, over London.

Feb 17, same one, follow up.

Feb 19, over Virginia and North Carolina.

Feb 19, over Penna.

Feb 21, over Newcastle, Eng.

Mar 2, over Cleveland, observed by MFS A. Wilson.

Mar 20, over Burtonsville, Alberta, Can.

Apr 3, over Texas.

Apr 10, over Arizona.

Apr 17, over Alton, Ill.

May 11, the daisy—over Seattle. Rumbled for thirty seconds after the explosion. Flash was seen 400 miles away, in Montana. A "geyser" of steam and water arose 200 feet in the air from Lake Washington, accto observer.

May 14, over Klamath Falls, Wash.

May 25, resume of meteors, N. Y. *Times* Mag.

May 30, another, but smaller and less noisy one, over Seattle.

June 16, at Adelaide, Australia, a "station" is being set up for the study of meteors.

June 18, the *Sandpoint Skyline*, Seattle, Wash., credits "Armed Forces Press Service" with the statement that—after an aerial explosion—between 2,000 and 3,000 meteoric stones fell on an area nine miles long by three miles wide, in or near L'Aigle, France, April 26, 1803.

June 24, another over Seattle, no explosion.

July 8, over Utah, Nevada, Idaho, Oregon.

July 11 (Wed. before), over Ashland, Oregon.

July 14, over Alton, Ill., St. Louis, Mo.

July 19, over Vermont.

Aug 8, over Montreal.

Sept 1, over Arizona, Calif., Nevada.

Sept 2, in Cordoba, Argentina, one fell and made a crater 130 feet across.

Sept 2 (Sun. before), over New Mexico.

Sept 12, over Virginia.

Sept 13, near Wheeling, W. Va.

Sept 18, over Calif., Arizona, etc.

Oct 8, over New Mexico.

Oct 17, over Miss., Louisiana, and Alabama.

Oct 26, Pruett

Oct 29 (Mon. before), over Quebec Province.

Nov 18, west of Graaff Reinet, South Africa.

Nov 20, over Los Angeles.

Nov 21, over Sussex, Eng.

Nov 21, four Southwestern States—Okla., Texas, Kansas, Colorado.

Nov 28, to the N-W of San Francisco.

Dec 1, observed by MFS Mitchell, W-N-W, over Long Island, N. Y.

Dec 8, over Erie County, N. Y.

Dec 10, over Okla.

Dec 29, over Seattle—broke windows.

Jan 3, 1953, near San Francisco. "Presumably plunged into the ocean". Seen 150 miles.

Feb 4, over Long Island Sound.

Two random pieces want dates and source.

A meteor may have set afire a "box and crate yard" in West Los Angeles.

AP reported a meteor over Plattsburg, N. Y., Burlington, Vt., Montreal and Ottawa.

PLEASE put the info on the clipping!

www.ingramcontent.com/pod-product-compliance
Lightning Source LLC
Chambersburg PA
CBHW081135300726
48982CB00005B/976

* 9 7 8 1 9 5 5 0 8 7 3 5 3 *